Jack and

in

The Banterless Breakfast Mystery

**Paulette Hallam and
Charlotte Moerman**

MAPLE
PUBLISHERS

The Banterless Breakfast Mystery

Author: Paulette Hallam & Charlotte Moerman

Copyright © Paulette Hallam & Charlotte Moerman (2023)

The right of Paulette Hallam & Charlotte Moerman to be identified as authors of this work has been asserted by the authors in accordance with section 77 and 78 of the Copyright, Designs and Patents Act 1988.

First Published in 2023

ISBN 978-1-915164-97-1 (Paperback)

Published by:
      Maple Publishers
      1 Brunel Way,
      Slough,
      SL1 1FQ, UK
      www.maplepublishers.com

Book Layout by:
      White Magic Studios
      www.whitemagicstudios.co.uk

Prologue

Walter

Hello. I am Walter. I am actually a big fat squidgy heat bag in the shape of a potato. Like all well-dressed potatoes, I wear a smart jacket and a large pair of superhero pants. I also have a big heart, a truckload of jokes and long wiggly arms, just *perfect* for hugging. Basically, I am an amazing friend.

I was made by a Grandma who loves her Grandson very much. I'm sort of saggy and not much of a looker, but Jack says I'm brilliant. I'm like a fluffy towel wrapped around you after a warm bath, or a home-made biscuit straight out of the oven. Irresistibly ace, so Jack says.

I'm just a normal kind of friend really. Only, I notice stuff, and I try to unscramble worries. So, if you're fretting or confused, or even if you've just stubbed your toe on a piece of Lego, I'm here to unmuddle, do a hug or say "let's smash this!" 'Cos sometimes you just need a little help.'

3

Jack

This is me. I'm Jack. My favourite room is the kitchen. The humungous table is ace for big family lunches and making dens under. Today I'm wondering why GP is so sad. Tara says it's because GP's lost her Mojo. I don't know what a Mojo is. But I would slay dragons to get GP's one back for her.

What is Love?

When GP spots a clump of buttercups, she always asks, "who loves a bit of butter then?" She'll pick one and pop it under my chin. Because there's a yellow glow on my skin, apparently it's *Scientific Proof* that I love butter. I'm not so sure. I think I prefer margarine. But I *love* Wotsits and my fingers turn orange when I eat them so maybe she's right?

GP says it's good to love. She loves a good crossword. And Jelly Babies, especially the purple ones. And a nice cup of coffee (she says, though it makes her breath smell funny). I once tried coffee and it was like a sort of poison that evil villains would make you drink,

"or the kitten gets it!"

GP is my Dad's mum and she lives with us. Mum once said GP came with the furniture but she definitely arrived with us in the car and didn't get put in the removal van. In actual fact, GP came to live with us when Grandad Star died.

GP is my most favourite person ever and this is kind of her story as well as mine. About how GP loved a special person very much but it makes her sad with a capital S that he's not around any more. I'm not bragging or anything, but it's also the story of how I tried to help her.

What is Love?

I love GP loads. But I also love Wotsits, especially sharing them with my best friend Henry Hamilton. And Fish Fingers. And Top Trumps and Walter, of course...

My big Sister Tara, she loves lots of girls' stuff. She's got Harry Styles posters all over her bedroom walls. (I don't think she's going to marry him, they've never actually met.) She also loves Eddie her *dreamy* boyfriend, her 'Candyfloss Fizz' pink lipstick, strawberries, ankle bracelets... Oh, and her mobile phone, of course.

My big brother, Theo, he's a bit less full of love and more full of teenage grump, though he *is* a big fan of Arsenal. He also loves loooooong lie-ins, listening to music in a dark room and creating a zoo of dirty underpants and socks on his bedroom floor. At least that's what Mums says.

My Mum, she's called Janice, she loves sunshine. And sheets on the line. And **pleases** and **thank yous**. Mint choc chip ice-cream, fluffed-up cushions and nice hot baths, "to wash you lot out of my hair." She also *loves to hate* her exercises, especially the ones called burpees. "It's all part of the **Battle of the Bulge**," she says, though I think it sounds more like you've drunk your pop too fast.

What is Love?

Dad. He loves hash browns. Doing impressions of someone called Mick Jagger which make Mum laugh. Old cars, *dark* chocolate and, "the proper consideration of all things Elf n Safety." Oh, and the Doctor Who theme tune which, he says, "reminds me of my youth," though it reminds me more of the Tardis spinning through outer space.

Last but not least, there's No-Banjo our dog. He's actually called Banjo but we're usually telling him off so he mostly gets called, "No-Banjo," or sometimes, "Oy-Gerrof-the-Sofa-Banjo." No-Banjo loves rolling in frosty grass, playing fetch, picking up stray socks and, basically, *anything* you can eat. Sometimes even things you wouldn't eat. Like pigs ears. And horse poo. Yuck!

Oh, I mustn't forget Walter. His real name is Walter the Great Unmuddler but I just call him Walter or sometimes Spud. When I was a baby I had no hair, like, forever. (Or at least until I was one.) Everyone thought I looked like a potato, so Spud was kind of like my family nickname. That's why, when GP made

Walter, she made him like a squidgy potato to be my special Spuddy Buddy.

Walter is a saggy grey colour, but he wears a smart jacket made from my favourite old PJs, 'cause all Respectable Potatoes have a jacket, right? He has smiley button eyes and long loop-de-loop arms which are ace for hugging and also pretty good at doing high fives. He's actually a lavender heat bag so is brilliant for snuggling with.

But he's also just like a Super-Hero. I mean, literally, he's got Superman Pants under his jacket. (Sewn on, so don't even ask if I looked!)

GP always says you need to wear your **big boy** pants to be brave which I guess is why Walter wears them. He's well brave. Oh and he also has tufty ginger eyebrows but don't let that put you off.

Walter doesn't want feeling scared or anxious to get in the way of life's big adventures.

What is Love?

He's helped me through some pretty sticky moments I can tell you by unmuddling my head. He's super cool, and he's my ROCK. I'm not saying I can get by without Walter ... buuuut ... OK, I guess I just *need* Walter in my life.

Even though she's super old, I guess that GP must be cool too to have made me such an ace buddy. Nobody knows her real name (well apart from maybe Dad). Everyone calls her GP except Grandad Star who just called her P. She wears crazy flowery dresses, carries around a secret stash of sweets and says things like, "take your coat off or you won't feel the benefit," which seems wrong because surely you need to put your coat *on* to feel warm?

As well as loving coffee and crosswords and funny sayings about buttercups, GP also says, when she's being a bit quiet, that Grandad Star was her **One True Love**. That all sounds very romantic, so I don't like to point out that she always says she loves *me* at bedtime too.

Grandad Star

Breakfast Blues

My tummy has a voice of its own. It's a right old grouch first thing. Most mornings, when I'm going downstairs, it full-on grumbles, "dunno about you but I'm *STARVING!*" I sometimes wonder if Luke Skywalker gets hungry-belly grumbles on Jedi-battle mornings or whether he just skips breakfast.

GP says, "breakfast is the **most important meal of the day!**" and I agree with her if I'm going down the stairs and smell bacon. (So does my tummy.)

The kitchen is my favourite room in our house. It has zillions of cupboards and secret drawers, a spider plant on the windowsill and a table the size of a swimming pool. All the important family stuff happens there. Like meal times, Monopoly and homework-that-needs-space. "This is a job for the Paper Mashey Team," says GP when I need help knocking up a quick Roman fortress before teatime.

The kitchen is always full of happy smells and noise. Always except this morning that is.

Most often, breakfast happens with three people talking at once, No-Banjo yangling for treats and the washing machine on top-volume bonkers cycle. Today it's just very quiet. GP, who's usually whirling around in her pinny, **Queen of All Things Breakfasty**, is just sat, silent at the breakfast table.

Perhaps she's doing daydreams. Or badgers have stolen her slippers. Or perhaps she's just feeling plain old sad.

Dad is wearing the pinny. It's not going well. He doesn't make a good Chief Breakfast Maker. I see that if I'm to shut up the tummy grumbles, I'm going to have to get my own Rice Crispies.

The radio is off and GP isn't taking any "snappies" like she loves to with her phone. Photos, she says, used to be, "rarer than hen's teeth," but, "now we can take ten-a-penny." Sometimes I don't understand half of what she says ... but that's better than her not saying anything at all.

GP is at the table in a world of her own, like when you have swimming pool ears and everything sounds far away. Her usual **Life's-Blood** cuppa has gone cold and she's not touched her marmalade on toast, which a certain bear from Deepest Darkest Peru would say simply wouldn't do. No-Banjo licks her hand (*slurp!*) but she just sits there, stock still, like she's playing Statues.

It's funny though, GP not doing anything seems to be making *us* all go wonky. Because it's usually her that keeps us on track. Everyone eats their breakfast ever so slowly and the clock tick tick ticks *really* loud. I feel like I did that time I lost Mum in the supermarket.

Everything's gone slow and weird and I wonder, maybe it's me who's doing the daydreams?

But then – BOOM - it's like someone's rung a bell and everyone goes ballistic.

"Come on kids! Eat up, clean your teeth and GET YOUR SHOES ON! The bus'll be here any minute," shouts Dad in a panic.

"Too late!" Mum screeches like a witch who's just had her ankles nipped by an angry Jack Russell. "You've *missed* the bus. I'll have to drop you off on the way to work."

This is not a good thing. Mum is a Sister

on a Ward. (Which doesn't mean her sister

Auntie Sue is waiting for her. She's told me

it's all about pills and spills and sick people.)

Mum works really hard. She's always tired.

And she's not going to be happy about having to drive us to

school first.

We scram in all directions like a game of Hide 'n' Seek. I

 run to my room for my school bag,

shoes and my all-important Walter card.

Whatever's up with GP, we'd better be making tracks. (And I'm

not talking about model railways.)

"See you later, Walter Tater!" I shout as I hurry out of my

bedroom.

"Better dash, before you're **MASH!**" I'm sure I hear as I fly

down the stairs.

The Car Journey

When Mum *ping pings* the locks, I scramble into the back

seat of the car.

Theo says you can't train cats to do anything but you *can*

train little brothers. I'm not sure that's true. I do all sorts that

he'd rather I didn't. Like taking the last custard cream from

the tin before he's home from Big School, sniggering when he's

got his headphones on and sings out loud, and sneaking into his

bedroom to do secret farts.

But letting him have the front seat on a day when Mum's about to explode? Totally no contest.

Tara scrunches in beside me and Theo's up front next to Mum. She starts the car and speeds off the drive like Lewis Hamilton. But instead of being all cross and crotchety, she says, "Sorry guys, what a crazy morning. We're all at sixes and sevens as GP would say. Just shows how much we rely on her eh?"

"Yeah," says Tara, "breakfasts with GP in a happy mood are much more fun."

"And somehow quicker," I agree.

"Like when she juggles eggs. As you do," says Theo, rubbing his chin and raising an eyebrow.

"Well, I'm not so sure about the egg-juggling bit," says Mum. "With Dave rattling on about Elf n Safety," chuckles Theo.

Dad is not their actual Dad so Tara and Theo call him Dave. Dad works in More-Gidges where one of his Special Jobs is being Health & Safety Officer on the side. This is like being Library Monitor at school which means you can stay inside when it's rainy at playtimes. In Dad's case, it also means he's gets

extra money, so Mum says.

Dad likes to take his role very seriously.
If Mum leaves her hair straighteners on, or
Theo drops his shoes in the middle of the floor,
Dad shouts out "Elf n Safety!" with a stern look.
Then we all shout it too and snort with laughter.
We even got Dad a special Elf hat at Christmas.

But today isn't a day for silly hats or laughter because

today, Mum tells us, is the anniversary of Grandad Star's passing

away which is why GP is so sad. Passing away means dying. Not

like passing you by in the street and seeing you later in the Post

Office, but the person going completely away.

"It's seven years since Grandad
Star died," Mum says. "He and GP had
been married for 42 years, can you
believe it?" That's a lot because I can
do my 6 times table and my 3s. "You

won't remember him Jack. You weren't even one," she says as she puts the indicator on to turn left into school.

The thing is, I don't remember Grandad Star himself, but I feel like I *did* know him because GP talks about him a lot. She says, "Grandad Star's not with us any more, but his soul and memory will always be with me. He was my **One True Love**."

The School Bus

Theo says I'd believe anything. When we first moved here,
Mum said I was old enough to use the school bus. Theo said
the SS1 sign on the front stood for Stupid School One. Duh, of
course I know that's not true. My new school is called Springfield
School so that's what the SS stands for, though I *prefer* to think
it stands for Space Ship One!

Every day when I get on, the bus driver Gary gives me a high five. He's cool. I think he's only disguised as a bus driver. We're actually top **Special Forces Accomplices** and are high fiving after catching a Great White Shark that's been terrorising the seas. Or performing a death-defying motorcycle stunt over a row of school buses. Or doing an experimental Space Walk while eating five king size Mars bars.

Today though, my high five is a bit feeble. I can't think what special stunt we might have achieved. I don't really feel like it. I think I might have lost my mojo?

I've been feeling odd all day. GP would say I'm off kilter. I've heard her say that before and I think it means feeling wonky and might have something to do with Scottish skirts for men.

Feeling off kilter?

I've been feeling sad for GP, and because I can't remember Grandad Star. GP says he was mad keen on fishing. I think of all the fish we could've caught together. And the golf we could've played. I can't play golf, but Grandad Star would've taught me. GP says he was also her **Number One Fan** when it came to her baking.

I *have* eaten lots of GP's cakes and I can vouch for Grandad's Star's good taste.

GP talks about him a lot but this is the first time I've seen her so off-kiltered. Perhaps it's the first time I've seen her on the actual day that Grandad Star died and went to Heaven. Or perhaps it's just that now I'm older it's the first time I've really noticed so much.

Of course, it really is a **Bad Thing** that Grandad Star died. But the good thing that came out of it was that GP came to live with us so she wouldn't be all alone. I feel a bit guilty, but that made me a pretty happy Jack. I can't imagine living without GP, she's such a big part of our family.

Even with her funny expressions (her "GPisms"), Radio 4 on in the kitchen all the time and the mobile phone that Dad got for her to keep in touch, which she actually uses to take photos **ALL** the time. She calls them her **Snappies**. Tara sighs, rolls her eyes and says *"Selfies!"* but GP just shrugs, holds the phone up and says, "Say Cheese for the Snappie everyone!"

23

I bet she wishes Grandad Star could see all the Snappies she takes. Or even *be* in one. Mum says that even though we - me, Tara and Theo - are her world, GP still misses her husband and her life before.

I think about how I felt when Boris our bunny died. I feel a bit like I need a wee just remembering. I can't go for a wee though, I'm on the bus and Gary won't let me off before my stop. (And weeing in my pants is simply not an option.)

It was really sad when Boris died because he wasn't very old. He was Tara's rabbit really. She got him for her 8th birthday. She looked after him really well, taking carrots and his special food to him every day. Letting him hop around our old garden. Helping Dad clean the cage. But one day, he just didn't wake up. It's like he went to sleep and then went straight to being dead.

Tara was upset because she really cared for Boris. I cried a lot too. I was sad that Boris had gone and we wouldn't be able to stroke him any more. But I was also scared in case GP went to sleep and didn't wake up. Or Mum did. Or No-Banjo for that matter. We put Boris in a shoe box and buried him in the garden. Boris didn't come with us when we moved though.

I sometimes wonder what will happen if I die? That really scares me but when I ask, Mum says, "right now, young man you are very much *ALIVE*. I can tell that because you are busy driving me **bananas** and asking me questions, like you *always* do. And you are drawing circles on my carpet with your toe. And you are gnawing your fingernails like a <u>*very-much-alive*</u> squirrel nibbling his nuts!"

Actually, I quite like her pointing out all these things I don't even know I'm doing. It sets me thinking in a different direction. I am like a kaleidoscope. One minute I'm all jarring shapes and colours, then Mum shakes things up, settles me down and all of a sudden I've changed track. Not worrying any more. I'll have to tell Walter I'm the Kaleidoscope King, I think before Mum butts in on my thoughts. "Don't worry Lovey," she says more softly and ruffling my hair, "you're not going to die any time soon, and certainly not on my watch!"

The only thing I ever had to care for, apart from giving Boris the odd carrot, was the class stick insect in the summer holidays in Year 2. It didn't go well. One day he was Harrold the stick insect. The next day he was just a stick.

HARROLD

I'm trying to work out how I felt about what happened to Harrold when Oli Perkins who's eleven and sits on the row in front turns round and is dangling over the seat back. He's so close I can count his eyebrow hairs and smell sweets on his breath.

"Want a Percy Pig?" he asks.

"No thanks," I say, "I'm not feeling hungry today."

"Suit yourself," he says and turns to face forward again. Rats, I think, maybe I should've taken one and put in it my pocket for later.

Home Again

EATING BAD GUYS...

...or Beans on Toast FOR BREAKFAST!

I got stuffed!

...with lavender and love!

Snuggle O'clock

CHAT TIME WITH MY FAVOURITE COOL AGONY AUNT

16:39

Spuds R Us!

"Alright Banj?" I say to No-Banjo as I walk into the kitchen and he *launches* himself at me like a missile. It doesn't matter how long you've been away, Banjo always gives you the biggest welcome like a long lost hero. Usually ending up with an all-over face slobber.

MISSILE INCOMING

SLOBBER ALERT!

"I'm not sure I needed a full facial," Mum usually says, "but I got one anyway!"

The Banterless Breakfast Mystery

Mum isn't around at the moment, she's still at work. Which is where Dad is too. GP would normally be in the kitchen ready to hand me a squash and a biscuit. (Or a piece of fruit if Mum's here.)

She's not in the kitchen today though, so once I've untangled myself from No-Banjo, I scooch upstairs to my bedroom to say hello to Walter. All day I've clutched my special Walter card in my pocket thinking, I bet Walter will know what to do.

Walter is no ordinary potato as you've probably worked out. He hangs out on my bed, just waiting to listen, dole out hugs and give advice. GP gave him to me the day we moved into our new house. I didn't even have a bed that night, just a mattress on the bare floor. I was scared about the gaps in the floorboards and what might creep out. GP said not to worry, I'd soon have Walter Wall carpets which made us both scream with laughter. Well, choosing him a name after that was a total no-brainer.

Walter is like a squidgy agony aunt, only cool. Well as cool as you can manage with big pants sewn onto your butt. Sometimes I catch him trying to look fierce likes he's ready to eat bad guys for breakfast. But underneath, I know he's a right softy pot. Literally, he's stuffed with the family's old socks and GP's lavender bag, so he's just one enormous squidge-cushion.

As I can't take Walter into school with me – I don't want anything *that* important getting lost or ruined – I have a special Walter card that I can pop in my pocket and secretly touch at any time to remind me of Walter if I need to be strong or brave.

The Walter card has a picture of Walter, of course. Every time I look at it I think how he's kind of a mini-me. What with being a Spud, which was *my* nickname, wearing PJs which were mine and having ginger hair. (Although *I've* got more on my head than my eyebrows at least.) Sometimes I think it's a bit freaky, actually. But then I look at him and remember I love him and how brave he makes me feel. Reading the card, printed with "Be Brave. Be Strong. Don't leave Coming Home too Long" always makes me feel happier. But now that I'm back with the real Walter, it's even better.

"How've you been today Jack?" asks Walter. (Did I mention that he talks, I surely did?) "Get any good Match Attax swaps at lunch time?"

"Nah. Didn't fancy Match Attax today. I took ages eating my lunch. The mash was dry and lumpy. Even the sponge and custard got stuck going down today, like a lorry in a traffic jam on the motorway."

"Told you, you'd be in the mash today didn't I?" chuckles Walter.

"OY!!" Cheeky!" I say back, giving him a stare like a cross kangaroo in hot weather, ready to box his ears. Which of course I would never do, but it doesn't harm to give him *the look!*

"I think I know why you weren't feeling hungry," says Walter. Walter always seems to know *exactly* what's going on in my head. "You're sad for GP today aren't you?"

"Blimey," I say, "did you *actually* go to mind-reading school?"

It was meant to be funny, but somehow I don't feel like laughing. We do a hug, especially tight. My eyes feel a bit tingly.

"GP and Grandad Star must've been such a team," I say after a bit. GP says they had such fun together. They had loads of friends and would always have people over for tea, GP baking a gazillion times better than Mr Kipling ever could.

She used to pretend she was a Top Chef and made up recipes of her own. She'd use secret ingredients that everyone had to guess. "Eat your heart out Heston Bloomingheck!" she says. I don't really understand that last bit, but the most important thing is that it tastes good.

"Did she tell you about the time she left a prune stone in her fruit crumble and Grandad Star broke a tooth?" asks Walter.

"Yeah," I chuckle. "I'm not sure I'd have wanted to eat that. For the tooth damage. *Or* the prunes!"

"Prunes," says Walter with a serious look on his face, "should be locked in a deep dark dungeon and nobody has the key. Or if you can't find a dungeon, they should just be left on the shelf at Tesco."

I laugh. Walter's funny. And right. Who even *likes* prunes? Well apart from GP and she can keep them!

GP, I remember. I want to do something to help GP. "What can we do Walter?"

So Walter and I sit and makes plans. And I tell him about being the Kaleidoscope King. And he tells me that I'm so right. It's often best to shake things up and look again with new eyes at whatever is causing you to feel sad or worried. Just like looking down a jiggy-jigged kaleidoscope.

"We need GP to do the Jiggy Jig thing," I say with a serious nod.

"Too right," says Walter with a matching nod right back at me. "Instead of being quiet and buttoned up in the corner of the kitchen table, we need GP to put on her **Big Girl Pants** and face up to her sad feelings. Talking about things always helps. If she can talk through her memories of Grandad Star then I bet a whole truckload of Curly Wurlys, we'll soon catch her in the very act of smiling again."

"You're so right," I say before adding, "do you think we should Make 'er, Walter Tater?"

And we giggle while I blush a bit wondering if GP's pants are flowery like her dresses. And also, just how **BIG** her big girl pants need to be!

The Bench

When we were little, Dad once made us a toy box. It was meant to keep the living room tidy. Only the toy box was not tidy. It was very soon in twenty pieces on the floor, spilling sawdust onto Mum's cream carpet.

Dad isn't very good at DIY. Tara said it was fine, Barbie didn't want to marry Office Executive Ken. She preferred Carpenter Ken. And Ken spent the rest of the afternoon shifting bits of wood about.

The Bench

He's not really made many things since. Apart from the kitchen table when we moved in. "Don't worry Love," said Mum, "it comes with assembly instructions."

"Oh good," Dad said, "my most favourite thing in the whole world is building flat-pack furniture," but I'm not sure he was telling the 100% truth.

Grandad Star, even though he was Dad's Dad, was ace at building things, so GP says. Like a bookshelf where GP keeps her cookery books, a knickknack rack in the shape of a big key, and a wooden carving of their first cat Mabel. He also made the garden bench that GP brought here from her old house.

GP loves sitting on that bench.

Peeping out of the kitchen window I can see GP is in the back garden, sitting on her bench, wearing a bright green cardigan. She is looking up at the sky and stroking Mabel, the wooden cat on her lap.

I wonder to myself, is Mabel her special friend like mine is Walter?

"Hello," she says as I sit down beside her, "I'm just telling Grandad Star about my day."

"I think it's been a quiet kind of day, GP," I say, looking at her sideways. And I realise that even though she's got wrinkles and her glasses are a bit wonky and her breath smells of coffee, GP is my most favouritest of people to sit and chatter with in the world.

"So it has," says GP with a slow nod.

I can't think of a single thing to say next. But it's OK, because sometimes just being quiet with GP is good too. But then I realise Walter's giving me a nudge and I remember what we talked about. About getting her into her **big girl pants** and making her talk out loud to me about Grandad Star. So I ask.

"Why is Grandad Star called Grandad Star?"

The Brightest Star is Grandad Star

The Bench

"Well ... Grandad is the brightest Star in the sky, remember?" says GP. "That's how he got his name Grandad Star and he is always looking down on us all."

This makes me think of the swimming pool. If you get into trouble, there's always someone sitting on the side on that tall seat watching over you. They wear a bright yellow T-shirt and no shoes, and make sure everyone is safe. That's what Grandpa Star must be like, I think, a sort of Elf and Safety in the Sky.

I'm smiling at the idea of Grandad Star in the yellow T-shirt and bare feet, imagining doing the *This little Piggy* rhyme. I wonder if I should take off my socks and wiggle my toes to make GP smile too.

But GP has her eyes closed and I think it's probably best not to.

Instead I open up Walter's loop-de-loop arms and put one around each side of GP in one of his happy hugs that always make

THESE ARMS ARE MADE FOR HUGGING

me feel better. She is a bit wider than me, so the arms don't go all the way round. But Walter seems to fit just fine.

Gently, I put my head on her knee next to Mabel, kind of like Banjo does when he wants something, like a biscuit or a wee. Only I'm not looking for one of those, just a smile from GP, that's all.

"GP, I know you're feeling really sad today. Mum told me why," I say. "You're missing Grandad Star even more than ever today, aren't you?"

I can't see if GP has opened her eyes, but I can feel her breathing, slow and steady, and I know that she's listening to me.

"Will you tell me about Grandad Star? What was he like?"

"Oh Jack. He was just perfect," says GP. "It's been seven years since he passed away but I still think about him lots. On birthdays and Christmases. When you bring something special home from school..."

"Like the fairground ride I made from match boxes that we thought would be ace fun for beetles on a day out.

Or the time when Mrs Roper had us all make pretend Viking poo and I brought mine home in my school bag!"

"Oh yes," winces GP, "maybe I'm thinking more the fairground ride type one."

I grin.

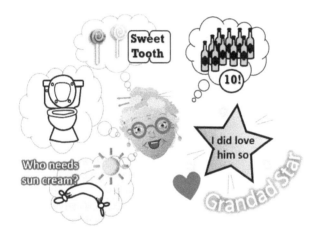

"And of course, this day is an especially special day. The day that he left us and went to Heaven. But you see, the thing I want you to understand is that William … Grandad Star … his energy is still here, all around me, and that helps a lot. I like to say hello to him when I sit on his special bench. He was my **One True Love** even with his funny little habits, bless him."

"Like what?" I ask, wanting to know more.

"Oooh. Well there was the way he'd whistle *Ten Green Bottles* while he worked. Or wear a hankie knotted on his head in summer. Scared of getting his head all sunburnt. Not scared of looking daft!"

"What else?"

"There was the special way he'd drink his tea. I knew exactly how he liked it. Two and a half spoons of sugar — sweet tooth — and really strong. Hardly worth splashing in any milk!"

"All the more for those that want," I say, knowing that GP loves her tea practically white.

"Don't get me wrong. He'd drive me mad sometimes too. *Always* left the toilet seat up. (Just like Theo.) Pick his teeth at the dinner table. And he'd suck on those awful lollipops as if he were a 5-year-old not 75. It was after he gave up smoking. No more cigarettes, but sugar coming out of his ears!"

I'm not sure I like the sound of sugar coming out of your ears, but smoking is bad, so maybe that's better?

The Bench

"Grandad would always say 'life's too short P to worry about the silly things.'" (Grandad called GP, just P as she never uses her first name.) "And now I know that it really was. I'd let him have his lollies for breakfast and all day long if I could just have him back with us for a bit longer."

Oh dear, GP's grabbed her hankie and is blowing her nose with a huge raspberry. I was meant to be making her feel better… The hankie, I notice, has a W in one corner. I wonder if Walter gave it to her?

"Silly old Rascal," GP is saying. "I did love him so…" (Another RASPBERRY nose-blow.)

Walter whispers something to me that I think I might try to say to GP. I hug myself tighter into her lap and wipe away the damp bits on my cheek on her skirt.

"It's so nice hearing how much you loved Grandad Star," I say quietly. "But I wish that love could be like the Baby Shampoo Mum uses… No more tears formula, eh GP?"

And there it is. A little chuckle. Bingo.

"Oh Jack," she says, "you make everything so much better."

And I sit up and we hug properly with Mabel and Walter squashed in the middle.

Perfect.

Later

Later, after I've finished my homework, like I always finish my homework with the sound of Theo's music wafting through the walls and Tara doing her sit-up exercises in the hallway outside my room, Dad calls us down for dinner.

I'll have to ask him to help me with my sums I think as I grab Walter, climb over Tara and thump down the stairs. I just can't understand ratios. It's too hard!

There's no sign of GP or Mum in the kitchen. Perhaps they're sitting together still on the bench outside? I grab a glass from the cupboard and slosh some water in it from the tap.

"Get on OK with your homework, Jack?" asks Dad.

"Well. Let's just say, if there are 10 glasses on the table," I frown, "and the ratio of water to milk is 2:8, how many cups of Ribena are there?"

"Uh?" grunts Theo as he makes his way in.

"Exactly," I say. "It makes absolutely *no* sense!"

Before anyone has a chance to scratch their heads any further, I hear the front door slam. Mum walks in and pops her car keys on the worktop. GP follows her with a pair of bulging white plastic bags.

"Is that what I think it is?" asks Theo, suddenly all interested, looking like No-Banjo with a bone in front of him. Only not wagging his tail cos he doesn't have one.

GP is nodding with a huge grin on her face. "The truth is," she says, "is that I've been rather *down in* **TIME TO DRAW THE LINE** *the dumps* today and I thought it was time to *draw the line!*"

GPism!

I'm not sure what drawing has to do with it but the kitchen suddenly feels alive again, all noisy and warm.

Probably helped by the lip-smacking smell coming out of those plastic bags. It's like the whole room and everyone in it is breathing a huge sigh of relief.

"So tonight ... as an extra special treat ... we've all got fish 'n' chips 'cos that was Grandad Star's favourite!"

"Egg and chips for you Tara," says Mum with a crinkly smile, 'cos Tara is a vegetarian.

Tara is laying the table and Theo's got the Ketchup, salt and vinegar out. Mum is humming to herself as she swills out the teapot and Dad has grabbed himself a bottle of beer. It feels a bit like a party.

Banjo is wagging his tail like a loony, and GP is taking wrapped-up white paper parcels out of the bags and popping one on everyone's plates. And as she goes around the table she is smiling smiling smiling.

"And last, but not least," she says, "here's the *Crowning Glory*..."

HERE'S THE CROWING GLORY

She puts down a large polystyrene pot in the middle of the table, right next to the Ketchup. It's not see-through but somehow the pot looks a bit green. I think I know what's in it. I think I might give Walter my portion.

"Come on everyone," she says, "I think this calls for a GP Special. It's our day to remember Grandad Star, and what better way to remember him than being together? I think that calls for a Snappie!"

"*Ugh, a SELFIE!*" groans everyone but with big smiles on their faces.

GP reaches into her unusually large pockets and pulls out her mobile phone, holding up the long-distance gadgety stick which also seems to live in the folds of her dress.

"Say Mushy Peeeeaaaas everyone!"

And we do. All 8 out of 8 of us. And I don't even care what kind of ratio that makes!

Walter's Questions

1. What do you thinks GP's name is?

2. Why do you think she doesn't like it?

3. What do you think a Walter hug would feel like?

4. If you had a Walter what would you talk to it about?

5. Why do you think Jack is helped by his chats with Walter?

6. Why do you think GP made Walter for Jack?

7. What do you have that you give hugs too?

8. How does Walter help organise Jacks feelings? Does he slow his worries down so he can sort them out?

9. Can you remember a time when you had to slow down your worries? How did it help you?

10. Who is your special adult or friend who helps you through worries either at home or school?

11. Do you think it helps to share your worries? What was the last worry and how did you deal with it?

Collectable Walter Card

Walter wishes and hopes you are happy and worry free.

But if you are worried about something, Walter says "Talk to someone."

As GP always says,

"A problem shared is a problem halved."

Lots of love and Hugs Walter x

Visit Jack and Walter, and make your own Walter card, at

www.walterontheweb.co.uk

Lightning Source UK Ltd.
Milton Keynes UK
UKHW020733250223
417592UK00008B/43